P9-DFZ-533

CORK & FUZZ

A Viking Easy-to-Read

by **Dori Chaconas**
illustrated by **Lisa McCue**

VIKING

VIKING
Published by Penguin Group
Penguin Young Readers Group,
345 Hudson Street, New York, New York 10014, U.S.A.
Penguin Group (Canada), 10 Alcorn Avenue, Toronto, Ontario, Canada M4V 3B2
(a division of Pearson Penguin Canada Inc.)
Penguin Books Ltd, 80 Strand, London WC2R 0RL, England
Penguin Ireland, 25 St Stephen's Green, Dublin 2, Ireland
(a division of Penguin Books Ltd)
Penguin Group (Australia), 250 Camberwell Road, Camberwell, Victoria 3124, Australia
(a division of Pearson Australia Group Pty Ltd)
Penguin Books India Pvt Ltd, 11 Community Centre, Panchsheel Park,
New Delhi - 110 017, India
Penguin Group (NZ), Cnr Airborne and Rosedale Roads, Albany, Auckland, New Zealand
(a division of Pearson New Zealand Ltd)
Penguin Books (South Africa) (Pty) Ltd, 24 Sturdee Avenue, Rosebank,
Johannesburg 2196, South Africa

Penguin Books Ltd, Registered Offices: 80 Strand, London WC2R 0RL, England

Published in 2005 by Viking, a division of Penguin Young Readers Group

1 3 5 7 9 10 8 6 4 2

LIBRARY OF CONGRESS CATALOGING-IN-PUBLICATION DATA
Chaconas, Dori, date-
Cork and Fuzz / by Dori Chaconas ; illustrated by Lisa McCue.
p. cm.
Summary: A possum and a muskrat become friends
despite their many differences.
ISBN 0-670-03602-1 (hardcover)
[1. Opossums—Fiction. 2. Muskrat—Fiction. 3. Friendship—Fiction.]
I. McCue, Lisa, ill. II. Title.
PZ7.C342Co 2005
[E]—dc22
2004013613

Manufactured in China
Set in Bookman
Book designed by Kelley McIntyre

Reading level: 2.0

Chapter One

Cork the muskrat looked behind

a thorn bush.

"Nobody here," he said.

He looked behind a pine tree.

"Nobody there," he said.

He picked up a small stone.

He dropped it.

He let out a big sigh.

"Nobody anywhere," Cork said.

Cork found a hollow log.

"Nothing to do!" he yelled into the log.

"Nothing to do!" an echo called back.

"Boring!" Cork called.

"Boring!" the echo called back.

"I have to go home now," Cork called.

"Can I come with you?" the echo asked.

Cork jumped back. He scratched his head.

"Well, okay," he said.

"I guess I can roll you there."

Cork pushed. The log began to roll.

"Oh-oh!" cried the echo.

The log bumped down a hill.

"Ow!"

The log bumped over a rock.

"Ow! *Ow!*"

It bumped into a big thorn bush.

"Ee-yow!"

A fat possum fell out.

"You are not an echo!" Cork said.

"What were you doing in that log?"

"Rolling," the possum said.

"And snacking."

He held up a shiny black beetle.

"Want a bite?" the possum asked.

"Uck," Cork said. He covered his eyes.

"I do not like beetles!"

"What do you like?" the possum asked.

"I like cattails," Cork said. "I like roots.
I like seeds."

"Uck!" the possum said. "Veggie stuff!"

Then Cork did not hear anything more.

He opened his eyes.

The possum had disappeared.

Chapter Two

Cork heard a noise behind him.

The possum popped out of the bushes.

Then he put something under a pointed leaf.

"What is that?" Cork asked.

"What did you put under that pointed leaf?"

"Just a little nothing," the possum said.

He stuck his nose against Cork's nose.

"My name is Fuzz," the possum said.

"My name is Cork," said Cork.

"Are you a duck?" Fuzz asked.

"Ducks go *cork! cork!*"

"Ducks do not go *cork! cork!*" Cork said.

"Ducks go *quack! quack!* I am a muskrat.
I float like a cork."

"I float like a rock," Fuzz said. "I am
afraid of water."

"I love water," Cork said.

"Do you want to play something?" Fuzz

asked. "Something *dry*?"

"We could play hide-and-seek," Cork said.

"Or we could play find-and-*eat*," Fuzz said.

"We find beetles. Then we eat them."

"Uck," Cork said.

"We could play catch-the-pinecone,"

Cork said.

He picked up a stick. He swung it at

a pine tree branch. A pinecone fell.

It landed on Fuzz's head. *Thunk!*

Fuzz gasped. Then he fell to the ground.

He did not move.

He did not move at all.

Chapter Three

Fuzz lay very still on the ground.

Cork bent down and wiggled Fuzz's tail.

Fuzz did not move.

Cork wiggled Fuzz's nose.

He wiggled Fuzz's foot.

Fuzz did not move.

Cork sat on the ground next to Fuzz.

Cork sniffled.

"I will stay here with you," Cork said.

A butterfly landed on Fuzz's ear.

"Shoo!" Cork said.

A grasshopper landed on Fuzz's paw.

"Shoo!" Cork said.

A caterpillar crawled up on Fuzz's belly.

"Shoo!" Cork said.

"Please do not be fainted much longer,"
Cork said.

Fuzz's eyes popped open.

"I am not fainted," Fuzz said.

"I was playing possum."

"Possum is not a fun game to play,"
Cork said.

"It is not a game," Fuzz said. "It is what
possums do when they are afraid.
Something hit me on the head.
I was afraid."

"It was only a pinecone," Cork said.

"A pinecone?" Fuzz said. "I thought it was a

giant buzzard bee."

Fuzz pushed the pinecone with his toe.

Then he picked something up off the ground.

He put it under the pointed leaf.

"What was that?" Cork asked.

"Just a little nothing," Fuzz answered.

Chapter Four

"I can teach you to play pin-the-tail-on-the-turtle," Cork said.

Cork found a long leaf.

He stuck a thorn in the end of the leaf.

"This is the turtle's tail," Cork told Fuzz.

"This is not a fun game for the turtle," Fuzz said. "He has got a thorn in his tail!"

"No, no, no!" Cork said.

"This is a pretend tail!"

Cork gave the leaf to Fuzz.

"That stump is a pretend turtle," Cork said.

"Close your eyes. Now stick the tail
on the turtle. I will find a leaf for me."
Cork bent over to pick up a leaf.
"Ee-yow!" he yelled.
"Uh-oh," said Fuzz.
"I am not the turtle!" Cork said. "Do not
stick the tail on me!"
"I am sorry," Fuzz said.

He hung his head.

Then he picked something up off the ground.

He put it under the pointed leaf.

Cork stuck his nose against Fuzz's nose.

"What are you hiding under that pointed leaf?" Cork said.

"Okay, I will show you," Fuzz said.

"But you will think it is silly."

Fuzz picked up the pointed leaf.

Under the leaf were three stones:

a red stone, a white stone, and

a shiny black stone.

"I collect interesting stones," Fuzz said.

At first Cork looked surprised.

Then he laughed.

"I knew you would laugh," Fuzz said.

"I will go home now."

"No, no, no!" Cork said. "I am laughing

because I collect stones, too! Come to

my pond! I will show you my stones."

"You live in a pond?" Fuzz asked.

"Yes," said Cork.

"Like a duck!" Fuzz said.

"Ducks live in ponds."

Cork picked up Fuzz's stones.

"Come on," said Cork, "and I will explain

again about muskrats and ducks."

"Cork, cork," quacked Fuzz.